For Laura, Harry and Lily, with much love IC

For James and Mollie, Bridget, Max and Ella CS

VIKING
Published by the Penguin Group
Penguin Books USA Inc., 375 Hudson Street, New York, New York 10014, U.S.A.
Penguin Books Australia Ltd, Ringwood, Victoria, Australia
Penguin Books Canada Ltd, 10 Alcorn Avenue, Toronto, Ontario, Canada M4V 3B2
Penguin Books (N.Z.) Ltd, 182—190 Wairau Road, Auckland 10, New Zealand

Penguin Books Ltd, Registered Offices: Harmondsworth, Middlesex, England

First published in Great Britain by ABC, All Books for Children, a division of The All Children's Company Ltd., 1992
First American edition published by Viking, a division of Penguin Books USA Inc., 1993

1 3 5 7 9 10 8 6 4 2

Text copyright © Lindsay Camp, 1992
Illustrations copyright © Clare Skilbeck, 1992
All rights reserved

Library of Congress Catalog Card Number: 92-16936
(CIP data available)
ISBN 0-670-84802-6
Printed in Hong Kong

Dinosaurs at
the Supermarket

Written by Lindsay Camp   Illustrated by Clare Skilbeck

Viking

Once there was a little girl called Laura whose best friend was a crocodile. He wasn't a very big crocodile or very fierce. In fact, he was rather shy, and liked being tickled. His name was Brigadier Simpson.

Laura's father couldn't see Brigadier Simpson. Actually, nobody could, and people were always stepping on his tail and sitting on him.

One day, Laura and Brigadier Simpson were in the garden, digging for buried treasure. They found a stone with a swirly round pattern on it. Laura took it inside to her father.

"It's a fossil," he said.

"What's a fossil?" asked Laura.

"Well," answered her father, "it's difficult to explain. It's sort of what's left of the bones of creatures who died out millions of years ago, long before there were even any people on Earth."

"Like dinosaurs, you mean?"

"Mmm," said Laura's father, turning back to his computer. "Something like that . . ."

Laura was very excited and hurried back to Brigadier
Simpson. "Daddy says it's a dinosaur bone! It's called a . . .
I can't remember what it's called. But it's definitely a dinosaur
bone. The dinosaur must have lived in our garden!"
She looked around doubtfully.

The garden wasn't very big.
There was barely room for the jungle gym.
Still, Brigadier Simpson was looking very nervous.
"Don't worry," said Laura. "He's not here anymore.
Daddy said all the dinosaurs died
out millions of years ago."

That night, Laura slept with the dinosaur bone under her pillow. The next day, she carried it everywhere. She even carried it into her bath, where she had a scary thought. What if the dinosaur wasn't really dead? What if he wanted his bone back? She didn't say anything to Brigadier Simpson, because she didn't want to frighten him.

Later, when her father finished reading her bedtime story, she asked him if he was really sure about all the dinosaurs being dead.

"Very sure,"
said her father.
"Now, go to sleep."

When Laura looked out the window in the morning, there was a dinosaur. He tried to hide behind the shed where the lawn mower lived, but he wasn't quick enough. Laura had seen him.

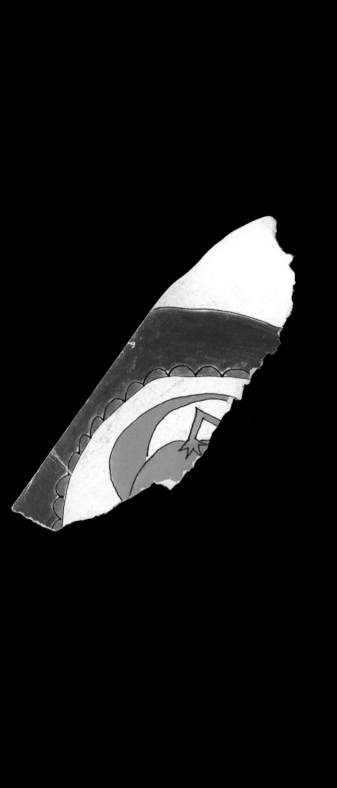

Laura got out her dinosaur book. There, on the front, was the same dinosaur.

Laura asked her father what the dinosaur on the book was called. He said it was a *Tyrannosaurus rex*, and it was definitely dead.

But Laura knew he was wrong.

Later, Laura saw the dinosaur again. This time, he didn't hide. And this time, he wasn't alone.

He was with his friends, and they were whispering together. Laura knew they were talking about how to get the bone back.

Laura wondered what to do.

If she gave the bone back, the dinosaurs might go away.

But she didn't want to give it back. It was her treasure. And she
was sure the dinosaur could manage without one tiny bone.

Laura decided to keep the bone. She still took it everywhere. But now the dinosaurs followed.

She saw them outside the supermarket. They had put their huge feet in the shopping carts and were whizzing around as if they were on roller skates.

She saw them at the library. They were stamping and roaring so loudly that it was difficult for Laura to choose her book.

When she went to school the next day, they were waiting in the playground. All day long they took turns peering at her through the classroom window.

But the funny thing was, the dinosaurs didn't do anything to Laura. They didn't chase her. They didn't jump out at her when she wasn't expecting it. And they didn't try to catch Brigadier Simpson and hold him prisoner until Laura gave back the bone.

A CROCUS

They just followed her.
Everywhere.

Then one day Laura's class went on a trip to the museum.
The dinosaurs came too. They seemed to like it at the museum.

Upstairs, there were big rooms full of glass cases with old things inside. Clack, *clack*, *clack* went Laura's shoes on the shiny floor. Clump, *clump*, *clump* went the dinosaurs' feet.

Suddenly, Laura stopped and stared. There, in a glass case right in front of her, was a dinosaur bone exactly like hers! It was a lot bigger, but it was definitely a bone from the same dinosaur.

Laura looked back at the dinosaurs. They seemed angry, showing their teeth and pushing into the room. Softly she asked the museum lady about the bone.

"It's called an ammonite," she said, "and when it was alive it was a little creature, like a snail, that lived under the sea."

Laura couldn't believe her ears. A snail! But hadn't Daddy said it was a dinosaur bone? And if it wasn't, why were the dinosaurs following her?

Laura turned around quickly. The dinosaurs were gone.

Laura thought that the dinosaurs might be waiting in the playground back at school. But they weren't.

And they weren't in the garden when she got home, either.
They'd definitely disappeared.

That night, Laura felt very sad. When her father finished reading her story, he saw she was crying.

"What's the matter?" he asked.

"You remember that dinosaur bone I found in the garden? I'm sure you said it was a dinosaur bone, but it wasn't. It was just a snail! The lady in the museum told me."

Laura's father hugged her, and said, "I'm sorry.
It was my fault — I was busy and I didn't explain
properly when you showed it to me."

"That's all right, Daddy," said Laura. She still felt sad
but she stopped crying when Daddy kissed her good night.

Brigadier Simpson, who didn't want Daddy to sit
on him, waited until Daddy left before
snuggling into bed with Laura. Soon
they were both fast asleep.

The next morning, Laura felt better. The sun was shining and Brigadier Simpson was already bouncing around.

Laura looked at him. There was something different about him. She closed her eyes, then looked again.

There was no doubt about it. Something had happened to Brigadier Simpson in the night. He wasn't a crocodile anymore — he was a dinosaur, just like the first one that Laura had seen in her garden!

Laura jumped happily out of bed. "Come on," she said. "We'd better hurry, or we'll be late for school."